The Bird Man of India
SÁLIM ALI
for Children

Zai Whitaker grew up in Mumbai, Maharashtra, in a family of naturalists, which was the beginning of her interest in wildlife and conservation. After college, she moved to Chennai, Tamil Nadu, and worked at the Madras Snake Park and later helped start the Madras Crocodile Bank in Mamallapuram, and the Irula Tribe Women's Welfare Society, Chengalpattu. She taught in Kodaikanal for 18 years and was principal of two schools. She has written 20 books, most of them for young people, on environmental issues. These include *Andamans Boy*, *Sálim Mamoo and Me*, *Kali and the Rat Snake* and *Cobra in My Kitchen*. She is the managing trustee of the Crocodile Bank, where she lives.

Note: The accent mark over the A of Sálim denotes a long vowel, which means that the name is pronounced 'Saa-lim', not 'Sa-leem'. He was very particular about this!

The Bird Man of India SÁLIM ALI for Children

ZAI WHITAKER

Illustrations by Rohan Dahotre

hachette INDIA

First published in hardback in 2003 by Permanent Black
D-28, Oxford Apartments, 11, IP Extension, Patparganj, Delhi-110092

This edition published in 2023 by Hachette India
(Registered name: Hachette Book Publishing India Pvt. Ltd)
An Hachette UK company
www.hachetteindia.com

SRD

Old place names such as Bombay, Bangalore and Burma have been used to preserve the historicity and historical authenticity of the text.

Subsequent edition/reprint specifications may be subject to change including but not limited to cover or inside finishes, paper, text colour and/or colour sections.

ISBN: 978-93-5731-194-6

Hachette Book Publishing India Pvt. Ltd
4th & 5th Floors, Corporate Centre
Plot No. 94, Sector 44, Gurugram – 122003, India

Typeset by Manmohan Kumar, Delhi

Printed and bound in India
by Manipal Technologies Limited

FSC www.fsc.org
MIX
Paper | Supporting responsible forestry
FSC™ C043100

To my parents Laeeq and Zafar Futehally

Sálim Ali, captured on camera in the middle of his typically hearty laugh

CONTENTS

Sálim Ali (standing extreme left) as Guide Lecturer at the Prince of Wales Museum (now Chhatrapati Shivaji Maharaj Vastu Sangrahalaya), Mumbai

A WELL-DRESSED SPARROW

A FEMALE SPARROW WAS NESTING in the stables, in a hole in the wall. While she was brooding – sitting on the eggs – the male kept guard outside, like an alert, well-paid watchman. Young Sálim (pronounced Saa-lim), who had just been given an airgun, shot the male. Soon after, he was surprised to see that the vacancy had been filled by another male, which was sitting on the same spot. Wanting to know more, Sálim shot him, too...and another replacement arrived. In all, he shot eight male sparrows over seven days and every time a new 'husband' turned up to guard the nest! This scientific observation by a nine-year-old boy was an important addition to the science of ornithology. Many years later, when Sálim was a famous ornithologist, his little notebook entry was published in an important journal on the natural history of birds. It proves you don't have to go into a thick jungle to be a naturalist and observe animals and birds. Our gardens and city parks are also places where important discoveries can be made.

Ornithologists? What are those? You must have guessed they are people who study birds. They start out as birdwatchers, with binoculars around their necks and notebooks in their pockets. Birdwatchers stumble a lot, because they forget to look at the ground. Their eyes are always on the treetops or the sky, hoping to spot the colours or movements of a bird.

Sálim's sister Kamoo was my grandmother. She told me that he once had a baby sparrow as a pet. It had fallen from its nest and been lovingly adopted by Sálim and his cousin. Being naughty and not properly potty-trained, it happily flew around making a mess whenever it felt like. Kamoo was asked to stitch a pair of shorts for the sparrow, which she did. It must have been a well-dressed sparrow, because my grandmother made beautiful clothes. But it was a problem getting them to stay up as, being a mere bird, it had no waist.

Kamoo was one of Sálim's eight siblings. In all, they were an army of nine brothers and sisters. But it was to be an orphan army: by the time Sálim, the youngest, was three, both parents had died. In those days, diseases like typhoid and jaundice killed a lot of people. Antibiotics and other life-saving medicines, which we commonly use now, had not been invented. Unlike most stories of orphans however, this one had a happy ending. The entire flock of children, all nine of them, were taken in by an uncle and aunt, Amiruddin and Hamida, who had no children of their own. They were not at all like step-parents in storybooks, but as loving and caring as any real parent could be.

Amir Manzil, their home, was a large, handsome house with arches and balconies and plenty of space, inside and outside. A good place for a small boy to wander about with an airgun. Gun?! Remember, this was almost a hundred years ago. Today, we do not like the sight of a child with a gun. It seems dangerous, and it is. Times have changed. Our cities are too crowded, modern guns too powerful, and animals and birds too few to allow the 'sport' of hunting. In those days, however, shooting birds and animals was a common hobby, and most naturalists started out as hunters. If you were interested in animals you became a *shikari* or hunter. The naturalist and hunter were often one and the same.

Shikar was a big part of Uncle Amir's life. Several well-known *shikari*s, many of them nawabs and rajas, were friends of his, and invited him to their special shooting reserves. These were stretches of forest where no one else was allowed to hunt. Today, many of them are sanctuaries and national parks where no one, not even nawabs, can hunt. Brother Hamid, much older than Sálim, was an officer in the British government, and Sálim enjoyed many exotic and adventurous holidays with him. Hamid was posted to remote and 'jungly' places, perfect holiday spots for Sálim. When, some 20 years later, Sálim became a serious ornithologist, birds had to be shot for identification, study, and to be preserved as museum specimens. He was a 'crack shot' even at the age of 70, thanks to his boyhood wanderings with the airgun.

It was an ideal boyhood. Being the youngest, he was wonderfully spoilt by his four sisters and four brothers, by Uncle Amir and Aunt Hamida, and by the domestic help, especially Nannoo the cook. In fact, Nannoo really helped create the Bird Man of India because he used to make him birdcages from old crates, packing cases and other junk. In these, Sálim, and his companion Suleiman – his older brother's son who was just two years younger than him – kept quails and partridges. Game birds like these were then common and unprotected, and often part of the menu. Sálim and Suleiman would secretly rescue them after they had been bought to be eaten. The little bird zoo was taken much more seriously than homework. Some of the birds had names, while others had to do without, and be nameless. Sálim and Suleiman would rush back from school to give them food and water and company.

The trip to and from school was done not by school bus but by tram. Life was certainly different then. Electricity and motor cars were still new inventions, and the radio not even dreamt of. The tram that took Sálim and his gang to school was pulled by a single strong horse or a pair of them. When they came to a slope, an extra horse was hitched on to the tram to give it more 'horse power'. These horses were often valuable animals, such as Walers imported from Australia, and had to be properly protected against the tropical sun. Many even wore sun hats, or sola topis, with two holes for the ears!

These were the days of the British Raj. Sálim grew up in a world where the 'whites' and 'natives' were separated as if by a barbed wire fence. Indians were not treated well in their own country. Trains, ships and buildings had 'Europeans Only' sections where Indians were not allowed.

Uncle Amir was a God-fearing Muslim. But he had modern ideas and beliefs. For example, he did not believe in keeping women in purdah. His adopted children, boys as well as girls, were educated; my grandmother Kamoo became the headmistress of a girls' school, and her sister Akhtar, a teacher. Sálim himself was not too interested in school.

He once joked that he had started birdwatching in order to escape homework. This interest in birds wasn't really shared by any of his friends and family, though Uncle Amir was one of the first members of the Bombay Natural History Society (BNHS), which had been started in 1883.

Sálim didn't pay much attention in class and his marks were on the low side. Nor was he very strong. He even had to be taken out of school for some time because of ill-health. For a while, it looked like he would always be weak and ill, and unable to lead a normal life. But he overcame this handicap brilliantly. He exercised hard and regularly, and ate healthy food with lots of fruit and vegetables. This made him a very strong and active man. Even at the age of 75, his swift walk left much younger people far behind.

But to go back to the 10-year-old boy, watching the caged and wild birds around him. His powers of observation were becoming sharp, and he would notice and study things that others missed. There is another famous 'sparrow story' about Sálim's becoming an ornithologist.

In those days, Chembur – now an overcrowded and polluted locality of Bombay (present-day Mumbai) – was a forested area, and every year Uncle Amir took his large family there for the summer holidays. This was also good sparrow country, and the common house sparrow would collect in large numbers to roost, that is, sleep. One of their favourite roosting places were the bundles of rice straw stored on trees to keep them out of reach of hungry cattle.

As it grew dark, flocks of sparrows would arrive to bury themselves in the cosy safety of these straw caves. Sálim and his friends would take potshots at the males with their airguns. They left the females alone, out of a feeling that you must be polite to ladies.

One of these males, conquered by the airgun, started Sálim's scientific career. It brought him to the BNHS, then a small organization, which was to play such a big part in his life.

The dead sparrow looked different. It had a yellow patch on its throat. Was it a disease, or maybe

some kind of stain? It looked like it had dribbled dal on its chin. The boys went in to consult Uncle Amir, who took a keen interest in their activities. He didn't know, but suggested that Sálim take the yellow-stained mystery bird to the BNHS.

During the British Raj, the BNHS was run by Europeans, or 'whites', and they were often very rude to Indians. Little Sálim felt he was walking into a den of lions. But Mr Millard, who was in charge, turned out to be a very friendly and helpful lion. He showed Sálim the thousands of stuffed birds BNHS had, making it one of the finest bird collections in the world now. For the little boy it must have been like finding a treasure trove: lines and lines of beautifully polished wooden drawers with bird specimens from the length and breadth of India, from thumb-sized sunbirds to man-sized cranes and flamingoes.

The sparrow had a yellow throat patch because it wasn't the ordinary house sparrow, but a yellow-throated sparrow. Mr Millard explained that birds and animals have a genus and species: just as we humans have a surname (genus) and species name (first name). For example, there are two species of crows in India, the house crow and the jungle crow. Both are from the genus *Corvus.* The house crow is *Corvus splendens* while the jungle crow is *Corvus macrorhynchos*; same genus, different species. Sálim greedily gulped down all the information that Mr Millard gave him. He had finally found someone who seemed to be as mad about birds as he was, no matter that his new 'friend' was many decades older than himself, and a member of the 'white' Raj.

BUSINESS IN BURMA

WHEN THE METALS TIN AND WOLFRAM were discovered in Tavoy, Burma (now Myanmar), it was a piece of luck for young Sálim, who was struggling with mathematics in college. He had managed to scrape through school. 'I could play cricket, and write essays, and that's about it,' he used to say. The Math Monster had totally conquered him, in school as well as in college. Now a life-saving letter had come from older brother Jabir, who had started a small business in Tavoy. He sold picks, shovels, nails and other hardware to tin and wolfram mines. Many of these mines were at Talaingya, a night-long sampan journey up the River Tavoy. (A sampan is a kind of canoe people used for travel in countries like Burma and Thailand.) Also, sister Akhtar and her family were in Burma, in Rangoon (now Yangon). Two good reasons to escape the miseries of college!

Eighteen-year-old Sálim left for Rangoon in September 1914, soon after the start of the First World War. India had been forced to join the war by her British rulers, and suffered heavy losses in money and human lives. It must have been an anxious journey, especially as their ship left Bombay harbour, because the German cruiser ship, the *Emden,* was operating in that area. The captain of Sálim's ship had daily boat drills in case of an attack, and there were always rumours going around among passengers that the *Emden* had been sighted. It is said that the real misery of war is rumour, and in this case it was quite true.

Being the tail end of the monsoon, the sea was still pretty rough. This was Sálim's first real sea journey; he had only done small ferry crossings around Bombay earlier. After reaching Calcutta (now Kolkata), it was another 40 hours to the mouth of the River Rangoon, which was quite crowded. The big ship hooted its horn at the smaller launches, sampans and barges in its way, and slowly chugged upriver into Rangoon town.

This was a major timber-logging area and huge fallen trees were being floated downriver, where elephants carried them to saw mills. In the next 30 or 40 years, Burma's forests would be butchered for their valuable timber. Sálim was lucky to have seen them as they were then, one of the last untouched jungles of the world.

Indians were not allowed to travel first class of course, so Sálim's ticket on the ship was for the 'European Deck'. This was a space on the deck of the ship reserved for educated Indians, Anglo-Indians and poor 'whites' who could not afford the first-class fare. Standing on deck as the ship got to Rangoon, he watched the Tseekai Maung Taulay wharf come closer and closer. At that small harbour was sister Akhtar, looking extremely happy even though she and her husband had recently lost their rented house and almost all their possessions in a fire.

The brief stop in Rangoon was delightful. In spite of the ravages of the fire, Akhtar retained her sharp sense of humour. She was witty and brave, generous and adventurous. These qualities made her an ideal pioneer's wife, which is what her husband Salah Tyabji was. Few Indians went to Rangoon without either staying or dining at the Tyabjis' home. Their hospitality, to the rich and the poor, was legendary in Rangoon. Salah, a very short little man, had many amazing war adventures. He narrowly escaped a mine explosion, missed a train which, he later discovered, was bombed, and walked overland to India after the Japanese occupation of Burma.

Back to Sálim. So it was time for him to get to his job in the little backwater town of Tavoy, on the river of the same name. Paddle steamships were still in use and in one of these he made the 24-hour hour journey to the mouth of the River Tavoy. From there, the *Yengyua*, a steam launch, took him upriver to Tavoy town, which was to be his home for the next nine years except for a break of about a year in Bombay. Burma, too, was ruled by the British government. Like the Andaman Islands, Tavoy was used as a criminal settlement during the British Raj. Much of Tavoy's local population was made up of ex-convicts who had chosen to settle there after being released from prison.

Here, the two brothers, Jabir and Sálim, established a business. But packing hardware and chasing customers for money was not to their taste. To everyone who knew the Ali family, the idea of them running a business was very funny. Jabir was a farmer at heart and his dream was to grow mangoes, which he did in the end. I still remember the juicy *aphoos* and *payari* varieties at his orchard in Chembur, and his orange beard after he'd 'tasted a few, just to make sure they are good enough to offer to my guests'. These Ali brothers and sisters never seemed to do anything without making a joke of it. As for Sálim, he often took off on Jabir's white pony to explore and enjoy the forest and rubber estates around them. He had no binoculars and there was still no 'bird book' to help him – he was to write the first one – so identifying or getting information about a particular bird was difficult. But he kept in touch with the BNHS and other birdwatchers in the subcontinent, asking questions and telling them about interesting birds he had seen.

From his early schooldays, Sálim had been a keen sportsman. In Tavoy he was the secretary of the football club, known by the important-sounding name of Tavoy Athletic Association. Many of the players were local British officials. The football field was an open unfenced ground and the members did their best to keep trespassers off it. The British judge Mr F.W. Scott was very possessive and didn't like non-footballers walking on the sacred field. One day, the milkman decided to take a shortcut through the field. Unfortunately for him, Scott Sahib was driving past, on his way to office. To the milkman's horror, the white sahib jumped out of his car and galloped towards him. Dropping the milk pail, the poor man ran for his life, while the angry Englishman emptied the milk on the ground. The milkman told himself it was no use crying over spilt milk, and went away. Later, at home, he got an even bigger shock. The Judge Sahib, no doubt ashamed of his behaviour, had come to pay him for the milk.

JUNGLE HOMES

IN 1917, SÁLIM LEFT BURMA to go on 'home leave' under orders from his 'boss', brother Jabir. He wanted Sálim to do a year's course in business and accounts. Perhaps he was hoping this would help improve their business, which wasn't doing very well at all. But then, as we know, the Alis had never been great money-makers. Thinkers, athletes, writers and social workers, yes; but they certainly didn't have golden thumbs.

Uncle Amir had died in February 1917, and Sálim must have wanted to share his sadness about this loss with the rest of the family. So, it was another ship journey and back to Bombay for 18 months. The business course at Davar's College was not enjoyable; Sálim's heart was not in debit and credit and balancing accounts. But as soon as those difficult two hours were over, he would dash off on his motorcycle to St. Xavier's College to attend zoology classes. This had been arranged by Father Blatter, the head of the zoology department. It was a great boon for Sálim even though he had to learn words like pseudopodia and anastomose. It gave him a good foundation in science, and the technical knowledge – especially about bird anatomy – was a tremendous help to him when he started his bird studies. Those long words and large grey textbooks helped him become not just a birdwatcher but one of India's great scientists.

After the business and zoology classes were over, Sálim would zoom over to the BNHS. He'd spend the rest of the day there, among its thousands of bird specimens. Several of the birds he'd seen in Burma had puzzled him and now he could finally put a name to them. A well-prepared specimen is a very good model of the living bird, but it has to be done just right. If done with care by a good taxidermist (a person who stuffs dead animals, birds and fish with a special material so that they look like living ones and can be displayed), it keeps the original colours and shape, and is a great help to ornithologists in the identification and study of birds. A bad specimen, on the other hand, can be very misleading.

Soon after his arrival in Bombay, Sálim began to suspect that the business course was not the only reason he'd been packed off to Bombay by Jabir. His family seemed to have another plan for him, a secret one. Sálim's sisters Ashraf and Kamoo had found a girl for their beloved brother. Sálim tried to make it clear that he wasn't interested in marriage. But matchmakers are determined people. They don't give up easily. The sisters were sure that once he met Tehmina, he'd change his mind. And they were right. After inspecting this new 'bird', Sálim completely forgot his earlier dislike of the idea of marriage. In December 1918 – the year the First World War ended – Tehmina and Sálim became man and wife.

In some ways, these two seemed as different as two people can possibly be. Sálim hated 'society' and social life and loved to wander about in forests, in muddy boots. Tehmina had grown up in fashionable society in London, and even attended a finishing school. Finishing schools were very popular with rich families in those days, and they still exist! They teach young ladies how to be stylish and 'posh': how to walk, say 'Hello' properly, how to smile (not too wide), how to laugh (not too loudly), how to nod (not too energetically), even how to hold a fork and knife. Tehmina had also been taught that while mixing tea, the hostess must say 'Excuse me' with a sweet (but not too wide) smile. Would these skills be of any help in Sálim's rough cabin in Tavoy?

As Sálim said, luckily finishing school had not finished off Tehmina. In fact, her heart had not been in this kind of learning at all. She was not the type who enjoyed small talk at fashionable parties. Like Sálim, she loved the outdoors, and reading, and a simple lifestyle. Along with brother Amir, who was going to join the family business in Burma, Sálim and Tehmina 'set sail' for Tavoy to start their married life.

By this time, even the optimist Jabir had finally accepted the fact that the mining project had failed. They decided to go into the timber business instead, which was booming. (But booming businesses did not always boom for the Ali family.) The plan was to rent, or lease, forests from the Burmese government, cut down trees and export the timber to India where the railways needed hardwoods like Burma teak for making sleepers and benches for trains. The railways were fast becoming the most important means of travel. Today, the Indian railway system is famous all over the world: this gigantic web of transport connects all corners of our country. The Ali brothers were excited about the new venture. But in this, too, they did not have the business sense to make it successful.

Their Burmese era was soon to end. Before it did end, however, Sálim had to make several 'business trips' to the jungle to find good areas to harvest timber from, and, of course, check out the birds as well.

Tehmina went along on some of these explorations, and she continued to be Sálim's birdwatching and camping partner until her tragic death after 21 years of marriage. Sometimes they slept in the huts of farmers of the Burmese Karen tribe, or in forest bungalows with no beds, running water or other comforts. But Tehmina had the talent of making the most 'jungly' place cosy and comfortable. In Tavoy, their simple cottage on stilts was converted into a delightful home. Tehmina had her own kitchen garden and poultry, and was able to serve roast duck and peas, both home products. Their home included 'General Dyer', a dog named after the British general who ordered the killing of innocent Indians at Jallianwala Bagh, during the freedom movement. They also reared a leopard cat, a tree shrew and a great pied hornbill.

Sálim had been lucky; he'd found a wife who loved the forests and their wildlife as much as he did. What is more, she never forced Sálim to take a regular job and earn a decent salary. Her own income, a present from her father, supported them and she was happy and proud that her husband was devoting his life to the study and protection of

birds. Not many wives would be so supportive of a non-earning husband! But Tehmina was not an ordinary woman, and her death in 1939 left a huge void in Sálim's life.

There was a story Sálim used to tell often. It tickled his boyish sense of humour and, at every telling, triggered his loud, croaky laugh. It is a tale, one of many, about funny mistakes in telegrams. Those born in the age of email and mobile phones may never even have seen a telegram. To send one, you had to write down your message on a form. The post office would then transfer it by Morse code to the post office nearest to the addressee. There, it would be typed out and pasted on another form, and the postman would jump on to his bicycle to deliver it. There was a lot of room for mistakes and misunderstanding, because the language of telegrams was English, with which the postal clerk was often not very familiar. So 'telegram stories' were always in circulation, somewhat like WhatsApp forwards nowadays.

Soon after Sálim met and became engaged to Tehmina, several people in her family were bedridden and quite ill with a bad flu. Sálim wanted to show them what a caring and helpful person he was, and decided to dash off a telegram offering to come and help nurse them. 'Shall I Come and Help?' he wrote. Tehmina's family was shocked to receive his telegram, which read: 'Small Income Send Help'. Poor Sálim must have had a lot of explaining and apologizing to do!

LUCKY MISFORTUNE

IN 1924, SÁLIM RETURNED to Bombay after several interesting but unprofitable years in Burma. He now wanted to get a job and give Tehmina some comforts. Their income from their families, was just enough to 'keep the wolf from the door', a rice-dal amount. Nothing left over for extras. Perhaps he was beginning to feel a bit awkward about not earning anything. Society says that men are supposed to earn a living, and support their wives and children.

But Sálim did not want just *any* job. In Burma, he'd realized his heart wasn't in business and trade. He wanted something connected with natural history, preferably birds. Eighty years ago, in the 1920s, this must have been like asking for an astronaut's job today. Natural history was a very new field and you couldn't hope to make a living as a naturalist or ornithologist.

Things have changed dramatically and I can think of many friends now who are naturalists. Then, the closest thing to a naturalist was the *shikari*, usually a British official with several eager 'native' helpers who did all the hard work while Sahib got the credit. Only slightly nutty, eccentric people went around looking at and studying birds and animals. There were a few: Hugh Whistler for birds, Mark Alexander Wynter-Blyth for butterflies, Frank Wall and M.A. Smith for snakes. But they were the exceptions. Natural history was simply not something 'normal' people were supposed to spend their time on.

Today, someone interested in wildlife and conservation can have a successful career. There are hundreds of organizations one can work for. Or, we can write about and take photographs of wildlife and habitats, make films, be a guide for ecotourists, carry out studies and surveys. Today, our schools and colleges teach students about the environment. Environmental science and wildlife management are important subjects, along with engineering and computers and medicine. So it is hard for us to imagine what a loser Sálim must have seemed. Like coin-collecting or stargazing, birdwatching was seen as a useless and rather silly thing to do.

There was another big difference. Today, we have good field guides that help us identify and study birds, animals and plants. We even have a choice of which field guide to buy or use. Birdwatchers nonchalantly say things like, 'Oh, I only use Flemming'. At that time, there was nothing. If you saw a bird or animal you didn't know, you could only write a letter to the one or two 'experts', usually the British director of a zoo or museum, and hope for an answer in a month or two. How frustrating!

Sálim's dream of studying birds would have to start from scratch; there were very few resources. In the years to come, he himself would write the first field guide to birds for India: *The Book of Indian Birds.* It would become one of the most famous Indian books ever. But at the start, it meant shooting, skinning, identifying and studying birds. Often, a specimen would have to be sent to museums and universities abroad for identification, because they had the best collections of Indian birds. In many ways, it was rather a mad ambition.

Fortunately for Sálim, his family supported him staunchly. His brothers, sisters and wife thought the world of 'Saloo' and encouraged him to stick to his guns, quite literally. So Saloo hopefully set about the hopeless task of finding a bird-related job.

He didn't have much of a choice of where to look. The only two centres of natural history in Bombay were the Zoological Survey of India (ZSI) and the BNHS. The latter was very new, a small group of people collecting and studying the birds of the Indian subcontinent. Funds for research were limited and it had a tiny staff. The ZSI, on the other hand, was a government institution with a network of field stations all over the country. So Sálim was excited when he heard that the ZSI had a vacancy, and that, too, for an ornithologist! He applied for the post at once, knowing that such a chance was not likely to come again. He was sorely disappointed when the job went to someone else, probably because Sálim did not have a university degree. Later, he often spoke to young people about the importance of 'that piece of paper'. They should get a degree, he said, however boring college classes may be.

For a while, Sálim reluctantly went back to the business world, this time working for his cousins in their cotton export firm, N. Futehally and Co. Like the Ali group, this part of the family was also not very business-minded and Sálim was astonished that the company had survived for so many years since it was started, around 1870. Sálim's salary, instead of going up, came down, from 150 rupees to 100 rupees per month. Fortunately, his days of being a 'businessman' were soon to come to an end. To his great delight, he was appointed Guide Lecturer in the natural history section of Bombay's Prince of Wales Museum (now Chhatrapati Shivaji Maharaj Vastu Sangrahalaya). The BNHS thought this would be a good way of educating people about natural history and conservation. The government agreed to pay for Sálim's salary.

This job at the museum saved Sálim's life in more ways than one. Not only did it rescue him from work he disliked, but the interview dates made it impossible for him to go on a tiger shoot that he had organized with Shums, his brother-in-law. Shums was married to Sálim's elder sister Ashraf. They had planned to go to Utnoor near Hyderabad (now Utnoor is part of Telangana), said to be among the finest tiger country in India at that time. Sálim was very disappointed that he had to drop out of this adventure because of the new job, but Shums went anyway, along with his cousin Azeem.

Sálim later got the news that Shums had been mauled and killed by a tiger he had wounded. Azeem, without a gun, had fought the tiger barehanded in an effort to save his cousin's life. He was badly injured, and hovered between life and death for several weeks, but survived in the end. He would vividly remember the nightmare all his life.

Happy to be in the world of birds and animals again, Sálim put his heart and soul into his new job. He taught groups of school and college students about natural history, showed them slides and models, and converted many to the religion of wildlife preservation. It was enjoyable, but more and more, he felt the gaps in his own knowledge of Indian birds.

His desire to study birds systematically grew with every passing day. He wrote an impulsive letter to the Berlin University's museum in Germany asking if he could study there. To his delighted surprise, he received an invitation from the eminent professor, Erwin Stresemann. The German ornithologist offered to take Sálim on as a pupil and teach him bird taxonomy, the science of identifying and classifying birds. Sálim accepted the invitation at once. Taking along 200 bird specimens recently collected by an ornithologist in Burma, he and Tehmina set off.

This impulsive, rather mad flight to Berlin – with a short stint, also, at the British Museum

(Natural History) – proved to be the making of Sálim. Not only was Stresemann an extraordinary ornithologist, he was also a truly great man: generous, dedicated, extremely disciplined, and a loyal and true friend. Both as a person and as a scientist, he made a tremendous impression on Sálim. There were other 'greats' in the Berlin University at that time as well, such as Bernhard Rensch, a brilliant zoologist studying the birds of the Sunda Islands in Indonesia. Sálim also met Ernest Mayr, who was to become one of the world's greatest biologists, and Oskar Heinroth, who was famous for his bird behaviour studies. It must have been exciting for all these bird people to be together under the kind and scholarly eye of Professor Stresemann.

It was in these laboratories and specimen rooms smelling of camphor and formalin that Sálim became a scientist. He learnt the techniques of foolproof taxonomy, which is the science of naming animals and birds. He learnt the importance of methodical and thorough investigation, and the dangerous results of making the smallest mistake. These were important lessons because Sálim Ali would go on to construct, or invent, Indian ornithology from scratch. And Stresemann could not have had a more serious and dedicated pupil.

There are many stories about Sálim's acute powers of observation and his scientific outlook. My father, Zafar Futehally, also an ornithologist, was with him in Bhutan on a bird survey. They came across some long-tailed sibias, a beautiful hill species. They puzzled Sálim because they had white patches on their foreheads. Sibias are supposed to have white only on their wings. Zafar excitedly exclaimed that it could be a new species or subspecies, but Sálim only said, 'Let's not be too sure until we have a bird in the hand.' The next day Sálim went out with his collecting gun and shot one. This 'bird in the hand' solved the mystery. The white on the forehead was pollen, from flowers on which the sibias had been feeding.

It was in Germany, too, that Sálim learnt about 'bird ringing', when birds are caught and a small plastic or metal ring is clamped on their leg. The ring has a number, which records the date and place where the bird was caught and ringed. It also has a message, giving a return address. The finder (usually a hunter) is asked to send the ring back so that one could know where the bird had been. Bird ringing, or bird banding as it is also called, began a new and important chapter in bird studies. It opened the door to the magical world of bird migration.

Heligoland is a rock island in the North Sea, an ideal site for bird ringing, located as it is on an important bird migration route. However, because it was barren and inhospitable, naturally no bird would take the time or trouble to stop there. German scientists solved this problem by creating a tempting bird haven with trees and shrubs and pools of water. A good picnic stopover for migrants! Hidden in the vegetation were traps ending in glass boxes, from where birds were collected for ringing. But the real attraction for the birds was the island's lighthouse. You see, migrating birds are magnetically attracted to lights, especially on dark and cloudy nights.

Sálim helped collect, ring and release the fluttering birds. He was not the only volunteer. Bird lovers come to Heligoland from all over Germany, and even from other countries, to witness this amazing sight. Well over a thousand birds were caught and ringed and released in one night – but many were not so lucky. They crashed against the lighthouse and lay fluttering, to die of exhaustion or get eaten up by stray cats, which enjoyed some free meals. Today, there are international regulations to protect migratory birds near lighthouses. For instance, soft nets must be put up around the light to prevent bird accidents. However, unfortunately, not all of us like to follow rules and some lighthouses continue to have unprotected lights.

Another bird killer is the aeroplane, which has sneaked into the birds' sky habitat. 'Bird hits' are quite common and a big bird – like a kite, or an eagle – can do enough damage to ground a plane, or cause a crash. As the human population grows and we invade the territory of birds and animals, these kinds of accidents are becoming more and more common.

A BIRD IN THE HAND

NOW WE CAN START calling him Sálim Bhai, as he was widely known. He is getting too learned and too important to be called just 'Sálim'. In a short time, he would stop being a Mr and become Dr Sálim Ali, because Bombay University awarded him an honorary doctorate. This was a rare honour, given after much thought and many meetings, to very exceptional students in a particular field of learning.

By the time of his death, Dr Sálim Ali was one of the Great Indians, a national hero. In many ways he was like another of our Greats, Mahatma Gandhi. Both Gandhiji and Sálim Ali were dedicated to, and lived for, an important cause. Gandhiji's was freedom for India, and Sálim Bhai's was birds. Both worked very hard for these causes. Both men loved their country and were proud to be Indians. Both were great readers and writers. Both loved to walk, and covered many hundreds of miles on foot – Gandhiji barefoot and Sálim Bhai in thick, heavy boots. Neither cared for money or property, good clothes or expensive things. Both had little hair, and a lot of nose. Both were great opponents of the British Raj in India. They liked the company of young people and were courageous, sometimes even foolishly brave. Both had a great sense of humour, and laughed loudly and sometimes toothlessly.

Still, all this future glory didn't help much right then, on Sálim Bhai's return from Germany. There was a surprise waiting for him, and not a pleasant one. The position at the Prince of Wales Museum had been cancelled! The government had decided to scrap the post of Guide Lecturer and Sálim Bhai was once again jobless.

On the good side, the experiences in Berlin and the British Museum had injected a new confidence and strength in him. He and Tehmina went for a while to Kihim, a coastal village south of Bombay, where her family had a small cottage. One day, while walking along the beautiful but scratchy scrub forest bordered by low hills, Sálim Bhai saw a weaver bird, or baya. Then he saw some more. He realized this was a colony of bayas, and they were nesting. For the next 3 or 4 months, for several hours a day, Sálim Bhai observed these fascinating birds. His notes and observations were to become famous.

Sálim Bhai discovered that the male baya is a wonderful builder, and the female baya chooses him as a husband not for his looks or colours (he is golden yellow in the nesting season) but for his building skills. Several males get together and start a housing colony, each one weaving a bottle-shaped nest with great care. When the nests are half-finished, a noisy party of baya ladies arrive to inspect them. Like women buying or rejecting vegetables in a market, they go from nest to nest, till they find one they like. The male flaps around, anxiously waiting for her decision. If she says 'Yes', she moves in and he carries on with the building work. Sálim Bhai also found that the male baya is not content with just one wife. As soon as one nest has been occupied by a wife, he moves on and starts another. He ends up with four or five families. This was the first time that the breeding biology of the baya was properly observed and understood.

It was a pioneering study, and the scientific paper he wrote on it has become a classic. The baya study also shows how powerful just a notebook and pencil can be, in the hands of a good observer.

So 1930, the 'jobless year', proved very fruitful. It was then, in the peace and quiet of Kihim, that he began working on *The Book of Indian Birds.* This has become every Indian birdwatcher's friend.

While watching the weaver birds hard at work, Sálim Bhai was weaving his own little plans for the future. 'Enough of this hunting for a job,' he decided. 'I'll just invent my own.' And he did.

Before Independence, some states in India were still ruled by the old royal families. These princely states belonged to rajas, who were mostly friendly towards the British government. One of the good things about these rajas was that they were interested in natural history. Several were birdwatchers, and friends of Sálim Bhai's. He decided to carry out bird studies in princely states and ask the rajas to pay the cost of these. He didn't ask for a salary, only his team's expenses. These would be low, as accommodation was usually in tents, and the skinned birds provided the meat for meals. The BNHS would lend him a couple of bird skinners and collectors, and in return get to keep the bird specimens in their collection. The bird team would also find out about the distribution and habits of the different species, and point out which birds were becoming rare and needed to be protected.

It was a grand idea. The rajas were happy to find out more about the birds of their states; so happy that soon they were asking Sálim Bhai to please do their state next! The Bird Man, as he was beginning to be called, was delighted, and so were the birds. At last, someone was taking a proper interest in them.

For Sálim Bhai, it was also an interesting peep into the world of Indian royalty. While a bird survey was underway in the lovely jungle of Balaram in Palanpur, the nawab of the princely state invited the local rajas of Gujarat and Saurashtra and Kutch to a stately dinner to meet Sálim Bhai. The arrival of each dignitary was announced by cannon fire. Sálim Bhai was amused to learn that the number of booms corresponded to the position of that particular person on the local royalty ladder.

The first raja Sálim Bhai asked was the Nizam of Hyderabad, who agreed and gave him 3,000 rupees for three months of fieldwork. One rupee certainly went a long way then. In the end, the survey took longer to finish – about six months – and the Nizam parted with some more money. Excited preparations were begun. Tehmina packed her little flower vase and other pretty objects with which she always made the shabby tents comfortable and attractive.

Looking at some old photographs of these bird camps, I can't help wondering how she could stand it. Their canvas tents must have leaked generously. Sálim Bhai chose the wildest, most snake-infested, 'scorpiony' places to pitch his tents, in some of the most remote and unexplored jungles in the country.

The Jeep had not yet arrived in the world and the only means of transport were special bullock carts that could negotiate those bumpy and uneven forest tracks. Often, Sálim Bhai and Tehmina chose the more comfortable mode of travel, and walked alongside the bullock cart that carried their gear and equipment. The bullock cart had one great advantage over the still rare motor car: unlike cars, the bullock cart was easy to repair and maintain. When it began to slow down, the bullocks were fed and watered, and speed increased magically! When the axle broke – as it often did on those terrible roads – the driver would run into the jungle with his axe, cut down a stout branch from a tree, and make another one. Once, Tehmina's sari had several burn holes in it from travelling on the Cochin Forest Tramway, which ran on wood from the nearby forests. It wasn't meant to be a passenger tram, but sometimes VIPs were transported on it. The VIP was often sprayed with cinders of burning coal that flew out of the engine.

None of the camp pictures show anything like a bathroom, so I wonder how Tehmina managed. The main dish would be a bird stew made from the day's collection. There were no other women around for her to talk to. The only conversation must have been about that day's 'catch' and plans for the next day. How delightful. But this rough and ready lady was game (and as we know, this small word means a lot).

Before starting the Hyderabad survey, Sálim Bhai had written to his guru Stresemann and his English ornithologist friend Hugh Whistler, asking them for advice on how best to do the Hyderabad state bird study. They gave him practical and thoughtful tips on how to get the most information from each specimen and from each day of the study. They stressed the importance of good observations in gathering scientific data on birds.

Whistler told Sálim that it was not enough to simply collect thousands of specimens. Collecting information and observations was just as important. 'All the time ask yourself the question WHY,' he advised the field teams. 'Why is the distribution patchy? Why is the bird in the sandy dry river bed and not in the cultivated [field]? Why is it in the roadside avenue and not in the forest? Let your notebook be just as important as your gun.'

Guesswork, warned Whistler, was dangerous. You may think you know that a certain specimen is a male because it has a red patch on the head... but that's not good enough; you must dissect it, and be absolutely sure. One should also look for 'incubation' patches, marks on the underside, which show that the bird was sitting on eggs. These tell us about nesting seasons as well as whether the male shares family duties or not. The age of the bird on the day of collection is also an important indicator of nesting seasons, rate of growth, and other natural history details. An experienced skinner, said Whistler, can look at a skull and tell whether the bird was a juvenile (young) or an adult. The juvenile skull is soft; it takes 3 or 4 months to 'ossify' or harden. Ossification (hardening of the bone) starts, and grows, in a certain definite pattern. Accurate notes about the actual amount of ossification, and where, would be very valuable in studying plumage changes in bird growth.

Whistler also told Sálim Bhai, 'I should like you to pay a good deal of attention to food, not of course the [usual] remark "insects" or "seeds", but to any special foods which are obviously being [eaten] by particular species and which may help to explain their distribution. It is advisable to take a good supply of test tubes and then stomach contents can be preserved...'

Whenever his bird surveys were praised, as they often were – all over the world – Sálim Bhai gave a fat share of the credit to these two loyal and helpful friends.

Let us look at some snapshots of the historic Hyderabad state survey. It is October 1931 and this jungle, Mananur, is the first camp. This is serious tiger country, and as Sálim Bhai walks out early in the morning with a Chenchu tribal tracker, they often see the fresh pug marks of tigers. While collecting birds they see several tigers. When it is time to shift to Camp 2, at Farahabad, Chenchu coolies are hired. Their wages: about a kilogram of *jowar* grain, which costs one-twelfth of a rupee!

Sálim Bhai and Tehmina are now camped on the banks of the River Godavari, in an abandoned cowshed which Tehmina, as usual, has made into a home with her little knick-knacks, and folding chairs and tables. In the local village, a story is going around about the strange Bombay-wallahs who have arrived suddenly, from nowhere: it is said their job is to shoot every kind of bird, and write down how it tastes! Soon, many village folk come to the campsite to offer their services as *shikari*s and guides, and one of them tells Sálim Bhai he can show him a crocodile that basked on the riverbank every day. Two days later he turns up again, telling Sálim Bhai the crocodile is visible. At least, he says, it is a black object that could very well be a crocodile. Sálim Bhai goes across and is horrified to see it is not a crocodile but a dead human body.

It is early morning and the bird team has just arrived, exhausted by travel. But Sálim Bhai allows no rest, and he himself has a superhuman capacity for work and activity. He expects everyone else to be the same. Specimen boxes are opened, guns cleaned, work tables arranged, chemicals for cleaning bird skins unpacked. By late afternoon, Sálim Bhai is off with his gun and notebook, leaving his assistant to shoot and collect the commoner birds around the camp. When Sálim Bhai returns, it is getting dark. He is pleased with the day's 'catch', and sits down to write his notes by the light of a lantern. Tehmina, meanwhile, supervises dinner and reads Urdu poetry, of which she has become very fond.

KERALA: FAVOURITE STATE

BETWEEN 1930 AND 1950, Sálim Bhai's life was one big camp. The Hyderabad bird survey was such a success that it became internationally famous as an example of how a natural history study should be done. When the Hyderabad report was published, letters came in from ornithologists all over the world, congratulating Sálim Bhai on his almost fantastic feat. It was the kind of work that could only have been done by a passionate naturalist, and only on foot. Today's naturalists like to fly in helicopters, or ride in Jeeps, with expensive equipment around their necks and in their pockets. Sálim Bhai's transport was his two sturdy, willing legs. It is said that he covered more Indian territory on foot than anyone has in Jeeps. He was a tireless walker and people half his age were often unable to keep up with him. His nephew Zafar wrote that during a study in Gujarat at age 60, Sálim Bhai would swing himself on to a camel's back – while his assistants, all much younger than him, would be looking around for a ladder.

After the Hyderabad success, it wasn't difficult to find money for bird surveys in other regions. The other princely states didn't want to be left out: if the Nizam of Hyderabad could have a bird survey done, so could they! Sálim Bhai's career was made. He camped and walked, collected and observed birds, in the princely states of Travancore–Cochin, Bhopal, Indore, Gwalior and Dhar, Mysore, Bahawalpur, Gujarat and Bastar. And in between, in 1937, he was in Afghanistan and in Kailash Mansarovar with the famous British ornithologist Colonel Meinertzhagen.

Apart from making several discoveries about the distribution and habits of Indian birds, Sálim Bhai was observing another interesting species: the Indian rajas. Like some of the rarer birds, they had a colourful life. With plenty of money and plenty of time, they could indulge in activities like shikar, which needed both these. And when a raja went on shikar, the animals had better watch out. There were hundreds of helpers to 'beat' the animal out of hiding and 'shoo' it towards the 'hunter'. There were others to skin the animals and carry them back in triumph to the palace. One raja-hunt could have as many as 200 helpers. Guns were cleaned and kept in tip-top condition; food and drinks were taken along to cool the raja's thirst and hunger. No wonder that some of them shot hundreds of tigers and leopards, and made the cheetah extinct in this country.

Kerala was Sálim Bhai's favourite place. He said this often. In his autobiography, *The Fall of a Sparrow,* he wrote that from among all the regional bird surveys he conducted between 1930 and 1950, possibly the one that gave him the most satisfaction both in the fieldwork and in reporting the results was the survey of Travancore–Cochin. Subsequently, it formed the foundation for his book *The Birds of Kerala*. He thought that the natural beauty of the region's hills was unequalled, that its ancient and luxuriant evergreen forests had an unmatched majesty, and that its flora and fauna were distinct compared with those of other parts of the Indian peninsula.

Kerala fascinated Sálim Bhai's scientific mind. There was a zoological mystery about the fauna and flora of the hills of the Western Ghats in Kerala. Why was it so very similar to the wildlife and vegetation of the Eastern Himalayas, western China, Burma and even Malaysia? Over 2,000 kilometres separate these locations, and yet they have identical species, which are found nowhere else. The problem has many explanations and arguments. Scientists love to fight over things like these. The biologist Dr Sunder Lal Hora came up with the 'Satpura Hypothesis'. He believed that millions of years ago, the Eastern Himalayas and south-west India were connected. Birds and animals evolved in this continuous landmass before they were separated by geographical changes.

The government of Travancore–Cochin had contributed 4,500 rupees for the survey and the Trivandrum Museum loaned their bird skinner. Sálim Bhai managed to save 2,000 rupees of the grant. Tehmina's accounts book gives the details: expenses for food for the entire camp; train and bus travel to and from Kerala; salaries for *shikari*s and jungle guides; cost of ammunition; and chemicals for preserving birds... All this and more came for 2,500 rupees – an amount which, today, would buy a few pizzas or books.

The richness of its bird life and forests made Kerala the best place for Sálim Bhai. He was especially excited by Thattekad on the River Periyar. As always when they set up camp, word spread that some crazy Bombay people were looking for birds. Word of mouth is often more powerful than the radio or television, so news always got around. A man tending his chickens in Parambikulam knew about the bird survey. When he saw a big bird swoop down to steal a chicken, he whacked it with a stick, and killed it. Being a railway fireman – trains were still fuelled with wood – he stopped his train near Sálim Bhai's camp and handed over the specimen. Quite by accident, Sálim Bhai had got one of the rarest birds in the world's ornithological collections.

However, when Sálim Bhai first saw it, he wasn't too pleased. In a rare instance of identifying a bird incorrectly, he thought it was a crested hawk eagle, which is common. The specimen boxes were getting full and finding space for it would be a problem. Fortunately, he did keep it. When the ornithologist Hugh Whistler was cataloguing the Kerala specimens for the British Museum, he thought Sálim Bhai was wrong, and said it was a Jerdon's baza. Well, that was wrong, too; it turned out to be the rare feather-toed hawk-eagle. It must have been a consolation for Sálim Bhai that he wasn't the only one this bird had managed to confuse.

Sálim Bhai's relationship with Kerala was a long one; he visited this favourite state every few years. He was dismayed by the rapid destruction of Kerala's forests after Independence. Corrupt politicians and greedy businessmen cut down valuable forests for the timber and plywood industries; dams for hydroelectric power drowned thousands of acres of priceless evergreen jungle; and poachers slaughtered tigers and elephants for skins and ivory. The wildlife-rich natural forests in which so many kinds of trees grew were replaced by monoculture forests in which only one species of tree was grown. The vast teak and rubber estates in Kerala may bring in a lot of money for the owners, but the birds and animals that once lived there became homeless refugees. To survive, birds and animals need a variety of indigenous or local species of vegetation, species with which they have evolved for millions of years and become dependent on. Just try and imagine a family of tigers living in a garden of rose bushes! It wouldn't work, would it? They would have no food or shelter and would starve to death fairly soon. Birds in monoculture plantations are like tigers in rose gardens: fish out of water. They find nothing to eat and nowhere to live.

In the 1970s, Sálim Bhai did a very great favour for Kerala. Silent Valley, that magnificent chunk of rainforest, was going to be flooded to dam the River Kundipuzha for hydel power. This was the home of many rare species of animals and birds including the lion-tailed macaque, which is a rare kind of monkey; the king cobra; and one of our largest flying birds, the great Indian hornbill. The trees and plants included rare species of great medicinal value. Silent Valley is a place of almost unearthly beauty and the thought of it being destroyed – for electrical power, which Kerala did not really lack – was unbearable for Sálim Bhai. Environmentalists all over the world were sending protest letters to the then prime minister, Mrs Indira Gandhi, and to the Kerala State Electricity Board, but it seemed like the battle was lost. Sálim Bhai used his personal friendship with Mrs Gandhi to plead for Silent Valley. This swung the balance and saved one of Kerala's forest treasures.

Sálim Ali with a young birdwatcher

SÁLIM'S ADVENTURES

DURING HIS SCHOOLDAYS, Sálim Bhai had visited his older brother Hamid, who was posted in Sind (now in Pakistan). Here he had come across the almost magical camouflage of the taloor or houbara bustard. This popular 'table bird' was shot from camel-back by desert folk, who seem to have telescopic vision. Not only are the bird's colours the exact shades of desert sand, but when it senses danger it plays another tricky card. Squatting low near a bush, it stretches its neck flat on the ground. From a distance, the bird would look like a dry cowpat. (In spite of all its efforts to hide, today the houbara has been almost wiped out by hunters.)

This got Sálim Bhai thinking about the camouflage colouration of birds in the desert. Desert birds were coloured so that they blended with the brown sand. It was like army uniforms in green, brown and khaki colours so the enemy finds it hard to spot a soldier. Another ornithologist had discovered that humidity in the air controls the amount of ultraviolet (UV) rays from the sun reaching the earth. Deserts, of course, have low humidity and this means a higher level of radiation. High humidity blocks UV rays. These rays bleach away colour, so the more UV rays there are, the paler everything will be. Thus, desert soil is pale, and so are the animals that live in it, to be less visible. But Sálim Bhai also noticed that desert birds that got a drenching in a shower of rain, turned the same dark colour as the wet soil. Their wonderful camouflage worked both when their habitat was dry, and when it was wet. Nature is indeed a wizard when it comes to the tricks of hiding from enemies!

For his desert study, Sálim Bhai chose Bahawalpur in Rajasthan, another of those princely states. The raja's British Resident, who controlled the state, as well as his 'Shikar Officer' were both members of the BNHS, and keen on Sálim Bhai's bird survey. So, in early 1939, the survey team found itself at the raja's breakfast table. To his surprise, Sálim Bhai saw a menu that listed the different dishes offered to First Class and Second Class guests! A First Class guest got two eggs, and a Second Class guest, one. Sálim Bhai waited in suspense to see what category of guest he had been classified as. He was relieved to see two eggs being put on his plate.

Sálim Bhai drove his team as hard in the desert as anywhere else. Often working in sky-high temperatures and for long periods without water, he managed as always to collect important specimens as well as make new discoveries. For a serious ornithologist, India was bird heaven; so little studied, and so much to be discovered. Almost every day, there would be a new discovery about the distribution of a species, or its feeding or nesting behaviour. Even though Sálim Bhai was a hard taskmaster, his assistants never complained. Maybe they were a bit frightened of him: he had quite a volcanic temper. Perhaps more importantly, he worked just as hard, or harder, than any of them. So they could hardly grumble.

His nephew Zafar, who visited Sálim Bhai during several of his surveys, including the desert ones, wrote: 'I found that all the members of the camp, which included two skinners and an unlimited number of "orderlies" of the Raj, were driven much harder by Sálim than any slave-driver would have dared to drive them. The team left the bungalow in the small hours [of the morning] with their collecting guns. The middle of the day was taken up in weighing, measuring and skinning the morning "bag". Another round in the jungle in the evening with notes being written up late into the night. As I got to know Sálim better, I discovered that an untiring thoroughness was part of his nature

and what he expected from others was only what he demanded of himself. He can also work longer hours than anyone else I know... At home in Bombay, I got used to hearing his typewriter tapping at five o'clock in the morning. This usually continued late into the night, with short intervals for meals, and a walk in the evening. The sight of the slight but muscular figure, carrying a stick, must have become familiar in the neighbourhood.'

Sálim Bhai was as fascinated by mountains as by the desert. He took every opportunity of trekking in the Himalayas, often with Arthur Foot, the headmaster of Doon School (in Dehradun, now in Uttarakhand). Although Sálim Bhai suffered from vertigo (giddiness some people experience when looking down from a high place), he didn't let this stop him, because bird life in the mountains is especially fascinating. The flora and fauna, the species of birds and plants, change dramatically as the elevation (height) increases. Each elevation or life zone has its own special species of birds. Sálim Bhai had seen that in Sikkim, Bhutan and Arunachal Pradesh, the life zones change from almost tropical (near the bottom of the hills) to arctic. He had led several expeditions in the southern part of the Himalayan Range. But what was on the other side of the Himalayas?

Sálim Bhai decided to go to western Tibet to find out. At the time, Tibet was an independent country. It was the home of little-known birds like the bar-headed goose. And there were sure to be other avian secrets in this unexplored part of the world. In 1945, Sálim Bhai set off for Mount Kailash and Lake Mansarovar. These are holy places visited by pilgrims every year; but his was, as Sálim Bhai said, an ornithological pilgrimage.

As they left Almora, the hilltops were ablaze with bonfires celebrating Hitler's defeat and the end of the Second World War. It was 14 May 1945. Sálim Bhai was disappointed because his close friends, Saif Tyabji and Loke Wan Tho, had been unable to join him as planned. His only companion was a young college student, the son of a friend in Hyderabad. And there was more disappointment ahead; this boy became so depressed that Sálim Bhai had to cut short the expedition. Perhaps it was the altitude; often, people are affected by the lack of oxygen. Or perhaps it was the sheer strain of covering 230 kilometres: 15 long days of murderous up-and-down marches with heavy knapsacks on their backs just to get to the border of Tibet, from where Sálim Bhai reluctantly decided to turn back. Not everyone is as tough as he was. But he, too, had his moments on this trek. The steep, narrow trail of loose earth and stones skirting cliffs of several hundred feet are not made for the faint-hearted traveller. At one point, he got too interested in the doings of a yellow-naped yuhina and stepped back to get a better angle with his binoculars. Behind him, he heard a small pebble fall...and fall, and fall. Looking back over his shoulder, he realized he had been 2 inches away from following that pebble.

Some more postcard-like glimpses of this historic expedition are available in Sálim Bhai's diary. I have rewritten these slightly to make them less telegraphic.

4 JUNE 1945

Making final arrangements for crossing Lipu Lekh pass, since the weather has cleared. Have decided we will have tsampa [a kind of suttoo or roasted gram flour] for lunch every day. It has been blowing hard: bluish light over the mountains. At 6.30 a.m., a strong earthquake for about 15 seconds. Rushed out, to see many landslides and avalanches. Dust clouds on hillsides all around, and loud rattle of stones and boulders bounding down. Some as large as a double-storey house.

5 JUNE

Preparing for trek to Taklakot (first village in Tibet); from there, baggage will go on yaks (incidentally, yaks love to eat the dry dung of the wild ass!). Plan to reach Gyanima around 15 July, after doing Mansarovar and Kailash.

6 JUNE

Did Garbyang to Kalapani at 12,000 ft. Temp. 39°F at 7 a.m. Heavy rain, and thunder and lightning of such force that every peal of thunder brought boulders hurtling down. Walked along narrow (3 ft wide) ledges with roaring rivers hundreds of feet below.

8 JUNE

Got up at 1 a.m., and set off for Lipu pass at 2 a.m. Had to take down tents, and capture and load our ponies, in pitch darkness except for one candle and one torch. No path, so stumbled and slipped on stones and boulders. Fresh soft snow an added challenge. Sometimes the ponies sank in and had to be yanked out, one man at the head and another hauling it out by the tail. On the worst bits they were unloaded and the baggage carried over. Reached top of Lipu Lekh pass at 6.15 p.m., temp. 28°F. I really suffered on this march, perhaps because of my bulging rucksack and heavy sheepskin coat. The ponies now return to Shangchin, and we switch to yaks.

10 JUNE
Three of the yaks refused to cross a wooden bridge and ran off, throwing part of their load. We carried the stuff over while they decided to swim across, in the icy, strong current!

11 JUNE
Camped at Sekang. At 3 a.m. a true Tibetan storm began. Our tents in danger of blowing away. Feet nearly, and water buckets really, frozen.

25 JUNE
At Ding Tso, about 15,200 ft. A small lake north-east of Mansarovar and local people believe it is even holier than Mansarovar. Its east shore is fascinating, with many islands of spongy vegetation. Dangerous to walk on, especially as there's quicksand here, too. Great crested grebes, brown-headed gulls and black-necked cranes breeding. Gelong warned me of the dangers of fooling around in this boggy bird haven but couldn't resist a grebe's floating nest. Began sinking in icy water. Made a desperate leap for an 'island', which was floating away, and only just made it. Shall listen to Gelong in future! He is very frightened of bandits and has reason to be. He was once beaten up, gagged, robbed and thrown by the roadside. Luckily, some people – non-bandits – passed by two days later and untied him.

Despite being cut short, it was a fruitful two months for Sálim Bhai. He discovered, for example, that snow finches nest in rat holes. But the price of scientific discovery is high. Along with the cold and exhaustion, there were terrible dangers such as storms and treacherous mountain paths where one false step meant death. And, to cap it all, Sálim Bhai was also accosted by a bandit, but fortunately managed to fool him. Poking around in the bushes for bird nests, he saw a sudden movement. There was a bandit in front of him, armed with a dagger in his belt and a gun on his shoulder. Sálim Bhai knew that escape was impossible. Doing some quick thinking, he whipped out his collapsible seat, the kind that cricket umpires use. It is a stick-like thing with a little seat you can pull out. Aiming the harmless object at the bandit and squinting to 'take aim', he click-clacked the seat open and shut, pretending he was loading his gun. Fortunately, the bandit had never been to a cricket match, and was fooled. He retreated sulkily.

Birds of Different Feathers

Have you spotted them?

YELLOW-THROATED SPARROW

LENGTH: 14 cm
WEIGHT: 14–20 g
HABITAT: Dry scrub forests, groves
DIET: Grains, insects, nectar

A small, dull, earthy-brown bird that is similar in size to the house sparrow. The male has a prominent reddish-brown shoulder patch and a yellow throat patch. The female does not have the throat patch and her shoulder patch is also slightly paler. Has slight hopping movements and a distinctive 'chirrp chirrp' call. This bird is found across India, from the southern parts of the country to the Himalayan foothills.

ORIENTAL PIED HORNBILL

LENGTH: 55–60 cm
WEIGHT: 600–900 g
HABITAT: Tropical moist evergreen forests
DIET: Fruits, insects, small birds

A large black-and-white bird with a huge yellow-and-black bill. Males and females are mostly similar in appearance except for the size. The males are larger and also have a bigger casque on their beaks. It is generally an arboreal bird and only descends to the ground to feed on fallen fruits and insects. It has a crow-like call along with loud nasal screeches. The oriental pied hornbill is found across the region from the Himalayan foothills to the North-East and eastern India.

RIVER TERN

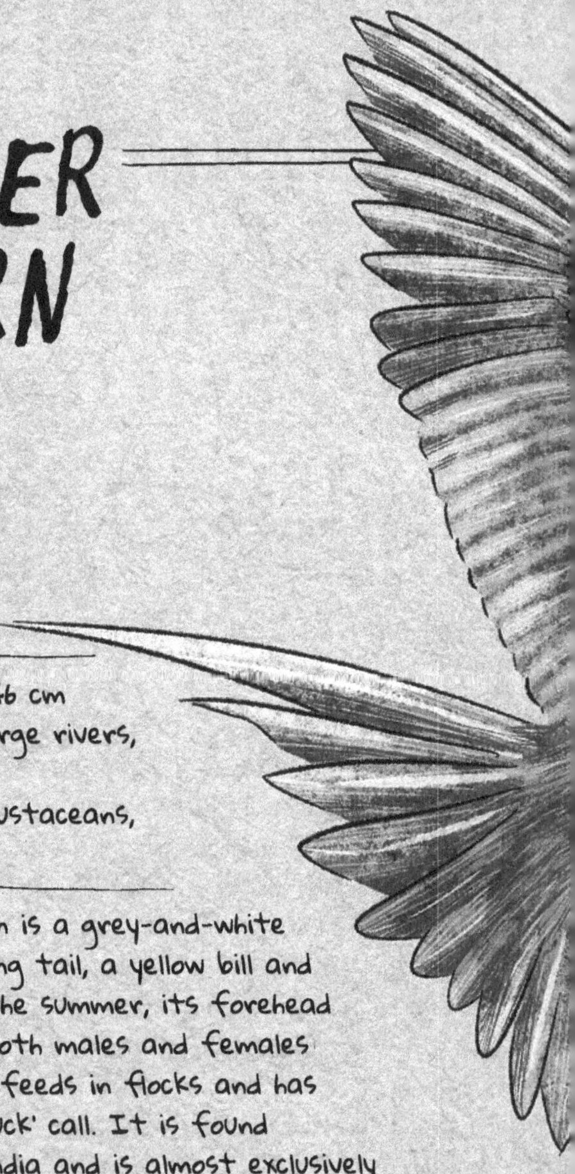

LENGTH: 38–46 cm
HABITAT: Large rivers, lakes
DIET: Fish, crustaceans, water insects

The river tern is a grey-and-white bird with a long tail, a yellow bill and red legs. In the summer, its forehead turns black. Both males and females look alike. It feeds in flocks and has a loud 'kuck kuck' call. It is found throughout India and is almost exclusively a freshwater bird. It feeds by first scanning the water for its prey and then diving to grab it out of the water swiftly.

LONG-TAILED SIBIA

LENGTH: 28–35 cm
WEIGHT: 40–45 g
HABITAT: Evergreen pine and oak forests, large scrub trees
DIET: Insects, berries, seeds

It is a grey bird with a long white-tipped tail and a white patch on its wing. Both males and females are alike in appearance. It makes a high-pitched tsit-tsit' call. It is mostly spotted in pairs or in small groups. The long-tailed sibia is found in the eastern part of the Himalayas and north-eastern India.

BAYA WEAVER

LENGTH: 15 cm
WEIGHT: 18–28 g
HABITAT: Grasslands, scrub forests
DIET: Seeds, grains, insects

The baya or Weaver bird is a small bird that, both in size and in appearance, looks strikingly similar to the sparrow, except that the male in breeding plumage has a bright yellow head and breast, and a dark brown face. They are found in flocks and make a distinct, neatly woven nest, which gives them their name. The baya can be found across India and neighbouring countries including Sri Lanka, Bangladesh and Pakistan. Its chip chip chip' call is also similar to the sparrow's.

BROWN-HEADED GULL

LENGTH: 45 cm

HABITAT: Coasts, large lakes, rivers

DIET: Fish, slugs, insects

Brown-headed gulls have a grey upper body and white underside. The head is chocolate brown in summer; in winter, the head is whitish grey. Its bill and legs are red in colour. The brown-headed gull arrives in India from the Tibetan Plateau during the winter and has a loud and screechy 'kea kea' call. It is a very gregarious bird and often roosts with other gulls. Being a bold feeder, it scavenges fishing harbours and boats of fishermen for its food.

ASIAN HOUBARA
(Macqueen's Bustard)

LENGTH: 65 cm
WEIGHT: 1,100–3,100 g
HABITAT: Deserts, sandy grasslands
DIET: Seeds, insects, lizards

The Asian houbara, also known as the Macqueen's bustard, is a domestic-hen sized, light brownish coloured bird. It has a white underbelly and black stripes on its slim neck. Males and females are alike except that the males are larger in size. It was almost on the verge of extinction due to hunting in the Middle East and Pakistan, but recent conservation efforts are trying to ensure an increase in its numbers in the wild. The Macqueen's bustard is a winter migrant to the dry and arid regions of north-West India.

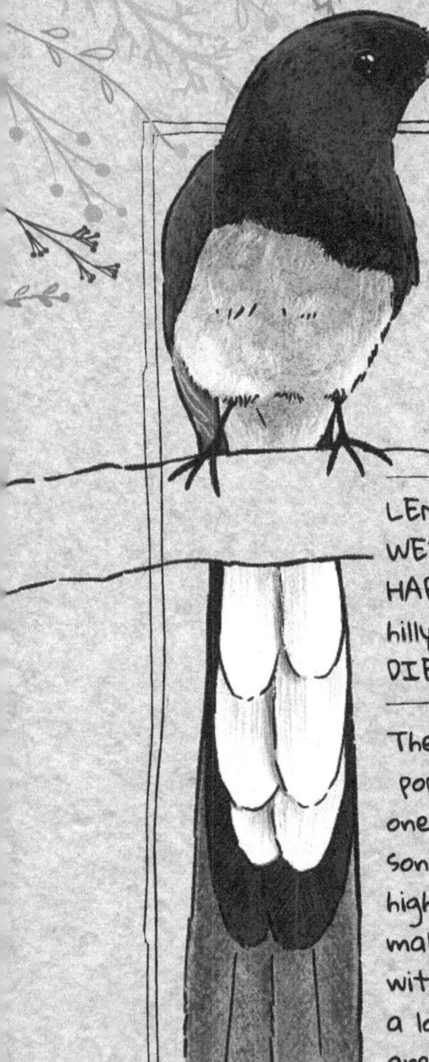

WHITE-RUMPED SHAMA

LENGTH: 25 cm
WEIGHT: 29–34 g
HABITAT: Dry deciduous forests, hilly jungles
DIET: Insects

The white-rumped shama, popular as a caged pet at one point of time, is a songster with a melodious and high-pitched whistling call. The males are shiny black in colour with a brownish underbelly and a long tail while the females are more greyish brown in colour. The females are slightly shorter than the males. The White-rumped Shama is widely distributed across south and south-eastern Asia.

FRIENDS AND FOES

IN JULY 1939, SÁLIM BHAI SUFFERED a great tragedy. His wife Tehmina died, after a small operation. It was not a risky or dangerous one, but hospitals were very different then, and surgery not as developed as it is now. Today, people have heart operations and are jumping about a month later, but back then, even a small medical problem could cause death. Several of our aunts and uncles died of typhoid, which is no longer a 'killer' disease.

Tehmina's death was a huge loss for Sálim Bhai. For 21 years, she had been his constant companion and friend: in camps in thick jungles, at a maharaja's dining table, or when visiting family and friends in Bombay or Germany or England. She played a big part in the making of the Bird Man of India.

At the time of her death, they were living, between bird surveys, in a cottage in Dehradun. After she was gone, Sálim Bhai did not want to face that sad, empty house any longer. Luckily for him, his sister Kamoo and her husband Hassan – my grandparents – invited him to come and live with them in Bombay. He moved to the beautiful, quiet suburb of Pali Hill. It was spacious and open, and at night you could see miles of starry sky. Today, Pali Hill is the home of another kind of star – the film star, and the skyline is crowded with high-rise buildings.

At 46 Pali Hill, next to the actor Dilip Kumar's home, Sálim Bhai was given a spacious apartment with lush greenery outside. Kamoo was a wonderful housekeeper and a loving sister. Nothing was too good for 'Saloo'. Also living there were Hassan's son Saad and his family, so the house had a comfortable, bustling, family atmosphere. At the same time, Sálim Bhai had no housekeeping worries. He did not have to think about things like ordering vegetables or repairing the car. He just had to walk upstairs at mealtimes, and tuck into Kamoo's delicious meals, which included home-made toffee and marmalade and pickles that no one has ever been able to duplicate.

Sálim Bhai could devote 12 hours a day to his work. He was finishing the *Book of Indian Birds.* The first drafts had been edited by Tehmina who had a 'feel for language'. The book has sold thousands of copies. Among its first users was former Indian Prime Minister Jawaharlal Nehru, who asked Sálim Bhai to sign a copy for his daughter Indira.

But I have wandered away from the title of this chapter. The move to Bombay had other advantages. Bombay was the home of the Alphonso or *aphoos* mango, Sálim Bhai's most favourite food. And it was here that he met Loke Wan Tho, the famous bird photographer who became one of his closest friends. He went along on many of Sálim Bhai's bird expeditions and bird-ringing camps. Loke's death in an air crash in 1964 was yet another great loss, both to Sálim Bhai and to ornithology.

The story of Loke Wan Tho is worthy of a film, or a book. Loke came from a very wealthy family in Singapore, the kind of family that owns huge mansions and businesses, and never has to scratch its head and wonder, 'Should I buy this; can I afford it?' But he was, as we shall see, not a typical millionaire at all, but a regular 'nice chap'. He was sent to school and college in England and then returned to Singapore to take over the family business, since his father had passed away. Soon after this, however, the Japanese invaded his city. Loke's family became refugees, and had to leave their possessions and flee.

They managed to get on a ship bound for Bombay. It was bombed by Japanese aircraft and Loke was badly burnt in the resulting fire – so badly that it was thought he had lost his eyesight. Rescued by an Australian ship, he was taken to Jakarta where he spent seven weeks in hospital. To the family's relief, his eyesight returned. They finally made it to Bombay.

Another visitor in Bombay at that time was Loke's very favourite English schoolteacher Jack Gibson, the headmaster of Doon School in Dehradun, and later of Mayo College in Ajmer, Rajasthan.

Through lucky chance, these two met up. When Loke mentioned to Gibson that he'd become very interested in birds and bird photography, Gibson put him in touch with Sálim Bhai. The two birdwatchers got on like a pair of chattering magpies.

Soon after they met, Sálim Bhai was preparing for the Kutch (now Kachchh) survey and invited Loke to go along. Loke jumped at the chance, of course. He proved to be an ideal camp companion. Like a good fruit, he was tough and hardy outside but soft and sweet inside. And he had a great sense of humour, which is always very useful when things are uncomfortable and difficult. Sálim Bhai writes in his autobiography that Loke was forever cheerful, even in bug-ridden *dharamshala*s or old cowsheds. Far from being a feast, these expeditions offered the same fare for lunch and dinner – dal and rice, and rice and dal! There wasn't much to

do after dark as the only light was provided by a hurricane lamp. However, in all the two to three years during which he accompanied Sálim Bhai, never did Loke whine or grumble. He went along on several bird-ringing camps both as a refugee in India, and after the war.

When Sálim Bhai shifted camp during a survey, it was done in old, battered, overloaded public vans and buses. They ran on charcoal gas in those war years, because petrol was rationed and hard to get. The old engines running on this unsatisfactory fuel often gave up, and 'passenger fuel' had to take over – everyone pushing with all their might. On one such occasion, on an uncomfortably hot and sweaty day, Loke turned to Sálim Bhai and said, 'You should really have your own Jeep.' Of course Sálim Bhai agreed, but wishing for a vehicle of his own was like wishing for the moon. He kept pushing the stalled van, and forgot about it. But Loke Wan Tho didn't.

Returning to Singapore after the war, Loke found that his Chinese manager had got on with the Japanese invaders and kept the business going wonderfully. He was richer than ever! He promptly sent Sálim Bhai the money to buy a Willys Jeep. This changed Sálim Bhai's life, making his work much easier, and less time-consuming and tiring.

And it was the first of many such gifts from Loke and his sister Lady Peng McNeice. Indian ornithology owes a lot to this generous and thoughtful Singapore family.

Very different from the gentle and polite Loke was another friend of Sálim Bhai's, Colonel Richard Meinertzhagen. He had been a colourful and adventurous officer in the British Army in Africa and his exploits are told in several books, some by him – like *Kenya Diary* – and others by his many admirers. He had won a medal for ending a tribal rebellion against the British government, by 'bravely' shooting its chief.

A more truly brave feat was fooling the Turks, enemies of the British, in the First World War. A Turkish battalion was preparing to attack a small British camp, which would certainly have been destroyed. Colonel Meinertzhagen used his wits to prevent this massacre. He made fake documents of a British attack in another area. Carrying these papers with him, he approached the enemy camp on horseback. As the Turks began shooting at him, he fled at full gallop with the Turks in hot pursuit. During the escape, he dropped the bag with the 'secret plan' and sure enough the Turks picked it up. Delighted at finding this top-secret information, they quickly set off in the wrong direction and the British camp was saved.

Apart from being an army man, the colonel was also an ornithologist. In 1937, he was arranging a collecting trip in Afghanistan and asked Sálim Bhai if he would like to go along as well. Having done some work in the Eastern Himalayas, Sálim Bhai was delighted. But getting along with Richard was a different matter. Loke and Sálim Bhai had hit it off immediately; but this friendship, like good wine, took time to mature. While Loke was always pleasant and good company, this colourful soldier could be quite a handful in camp, and enjoyed terrorizing the 'natives'. Loke and he had opposite attitudes to the political situation in India. While Loke sympathized with the Indian struggle for independence, Meinertzhagen believed India was much better off under the British. However, he soon realized that Sálim Bhai was a strong nationalist and was not very polite when he felt strongly about something. They both realized early that the other would not change his views, so the subject was not brought up. They put aside their differences and got on with the business of collecting, skinning and studying birds, something they both loved.

Richard and Sálim Bhai wanted to make the best use of being in the bird paradise of Afghanistan. They set off early every morning, in different directions. Each had a local *shikari* with him, both for collection as well as for protection; this again was 'bandit' country. Colonel Meinertzhagen was studying the feather lice (mallophaga) of birds. Feather lice are an important part of bird taxonomy, identification and classification, because each species of lice lives only on a certain species of bird. You can identify a bird by the species of mallophaga on its feathers. They came back with a wonderful collection and much interesting and new data.

However, Richard Meinertzhagen is now a dishonoured name among the ornithologist community. In the 1990s, he was proved to be a scientific fraud; and Science, for obvious reasons, does not easily forgive cheaters. It turns out that he had committed a serious crime, by 'cooking up' scientific data in order to gain fame and glory in the world of ornithology. Listen to this story.

The rare forest spotted owlet was thought to be extinct. But it was suddenly rediscovered in 1986, causing much excitement among birders. One of the important specimens being used to study this bird and its distribution had been collected by Colonel

Meinertzhagen in 1914. Another ornithologist, Dr Pamela Rasmussen, an expert on the birds of the Indian subcontinent, became suspicious about this specimen. By then, Meinertzhagen's reputation had become a little muddy, and one or two of his data had been proved to be fictitious. He had also, it was said, pinched specimens from other collections and passed them off as his own, with false information about the date and area of collection. Dr Rasmussen was writing an important book about the birds of this region, and wanted to be 100 per cent sure that Meinertzhagen's information was reliable. Had this rare owlet really been found on the River Tapti?

Now, each collector's team has its own style of preparing a bird skin. On examining the specimen at the British Museum, Rasmussen and her colleagues found that it was, indeed, not a typical Meinertzhagen specimen. But that was not all. To their shock and surprise, they found it had been altered. It had been opened up, new stuffing put in, and stitched up again, all obviously to conceal the identity of the original collector.

Through meticulous study of the British Museum's data and various forensic tests, it was discovered that this 'phony' specimen had actually been collected at quite another location some 15 years earlier, by the ornithologist Davidson. Meinertzhagen had pinched it to gain ornithological glory. The case was finally clinched when some of the original Davidson stuffing was found in one of the hidden joints of the specimen. This was compared to the fibres in the stuffing in another of Davidson's specimens: the fibres were identical. And, thus, one of the biggest frauds in ornithology came to light. It is a good thing that Sálim Bhai did not live to see the sad end of Meinertzhagen's reputation.

There were many other important friendships in Sálim Bhai's life. Dr S.D. Ripley of the Smithsonian Institution in Washington was another bird-study buddy. He and Sálim Bhai together wrote the 10-volume *Handbook of the Birds of India and Pakistan.* Closer home, he had his nephew Zafar and J.C. Daniel, both active in the BNHS. They supported and helped Sálim Bhai in many ways. Perhaps their main contribution to Sálim Bhai was to allow him to keep going, and not let people put a spoke in the wheel of his work.

As Sálim Bhai became more and more famous, there grew around him some jealousy and envy. He was getting prizes and awards from all over the world – India, Britain, the USA, the USSR, the Netherlands, Bangladesh...to name only a few.

In India, he received the Padma Bhushan in 1958 and the Padma Vibhushan in 1976, the year he was honoured with the J. Paul Getty International Prize for Wildlife Conservation, along with 50,000 US dollars, which he gave to the BNHS. So, naturally, some malicious people tried to give him a hard time. But most of the time he was too busy to notice, or care. And he had plenty of good friends to neutralize the effect of his enemies.

THE MAGIC RING

EARLY NATURALISTS SPENT A LOT of time scratching their heads and wondering. They did not have the solid body of scientific work that we have today. We can trot off to a library and find out about something as remote as, say, the bushmaster of South America or the megapode of Papua New Guinea. Or we can get on the internet and go click-click-click and read the latest scientific discoveries about otters and ostriches, elephants and eels. But this was not always so. In fact, it is only in the last hundred years that the secrets about birds and animals have been unlocked.

One of the mysteries that caused much head-scratching and mumbling through learned beards was bird migration. Large flocks of thousands of birds left a place and came back a year later around the same time, sometimes on the very same day. Where did they go and how did they find their way back? Some early naturalists believed they hid in the bottom of the sea, to rise like the phoenix in Greek legends.

Of course, scientific study and discovery had progressed much further by Sálim Bhai's time. By then, naturalists knew that many species of birds, big and small, fly very long distances every year to escape cold winters, to lay their eggs and raise their chicks in the comfort of a warm land. After all, who wants to be in Siberia in winter! Like all tourists, birds want warmth and good food and a comfortable place (at reasonable prices). Some fly thousands of kilometres – each way – to and from their winter resting place.

Yet, how do birds find their way to a specific spot on the other side of the world, year after year? Like computer-programmed objects, they fly thousands of kilometres and land at a specific lake or forest or river. Their timing, too, is perfect: migrants are extremely punctual, unlike many of us, and arrive within a day or two of their previous year's arrival. Without watches or computers or travel agents, how do they do it? Why don't they lose their way, or die of exhaustion?

It was once thought that migration was a 'taught' behaviour, and that bird parents guided their young on these long journeys. But in many species of birds, the young make their first migratory journey alone, without their parents. Sálim Bhai often gave the example of the cuckoo in Europe, and he once told a journalist:

> The cuckoo is what is called a brood parasite. It lays its eggs in the nests of other species, and just forgets about it. The young are hatched out and brought up by the foster parents. Now, in the UK, the cuckoo, soon after laying its eggs, migrates to Africa. The young are brought up by foster parents who themselves are non-migratory birds. They do not migrate and therefore they cannot teach their foster birdlings anything about migration. Yet, remarkably enough, as soon as the young cuckoo is able to fly, it flies off to join its parents in Africa – may be as much as 6,500 kilometres.

Migration is therefore not a behaviour that is taught by parents. It is caused by strong genetic or inborn instincts that all animals – from molluscs to elephants – share. Like a good computer program, instinct guides them to food and friends, keeps them away from danger, and prevents them from getting lost as they roam miles and miles in different directions.

There are two seasons of bird 'travel' to and from India every year. Millions of birds belonging to about 300 species fly thousands of kilometres to get to their nesting places and return in the spring when the weather warms up. A flock of migrating birds, sometimes several thousand strong, is an unforgettable sight. This is also the time when otherwise solitary birds are seen together. The marsh harrier, for example, is usually seen individually or in pairs, but during a survey in Afghanistan, Sálim Bhai saw a large flock of them arriving and settling in a ploughed field as it was getting dark. Having come all the way from India, they were obviously exhausted. But they were off again at daybreak.

Ornithologists in many countries had begun studying bird migration by ringing birds. Around 1960, Sálim Bhai, too, made a start with his team from the BNHS. A small aluminium or plastic ring – too small and light to handicap the bird – is clamped on the bird's foot. On the ring is a message asking the finder of the bird to return the ring to a particular address, such as the BNHS. They are also asked to name the place, date and time the bird was found. The bird-ringing camps he had participated in – in Heligoland, Germany – had given Sálim Bhai useful training in this area. A few bird-ringing camps, and their results, showed that it should be done on a larger scale. But there was the usual, small problem. Money. For a while it looked pretty unhopeful. But in the end, it did work out, thanks, funnily enough, to a lowly virus.

A strange viral disease had broken out in Shimoga district of Karnataka state, and was affecting humans and monkeys. It was new to Indian doctors, and no one could figure out exactly what it was or how to cure it. It became even more mysterious when scientists at the Pune Virus Research Centre, peering through their microscopes, discovered that it came from western Siberia. There, it caused a disease known as Russian Spring–Summer Encephalitis, very much like the Shimoga sickness. But how did this Siberian virus get to Karnataka?

The World Health Organization (WHO) wanted to find out, and it asked Sálim Bhai and the BNHS to help. The ticks and other parasites carrying this virus had been brought over, perhaps from Siberia. How? Could migratory birds be the culprits? Many winter migrants in India came from Siberia, so it was likely. Well, Sálim Bhai was only too happy to help find out, and he was invited to a WHO meeting in Geneva, Switzerland, to make all the arrangements. And in this way, bird ringing (or bird banding) began in India. Sálim Bhai would certainly collect ticks and other parasites for the WHO. At the same time, he would be able to clamp on the magic ring that would tell the story of bird migration to and from India.

The first area chosen for setting up a bird-ringing camp was the Rann of Kachchh. Why, of all places, the uncomfortable desert of Kachchh? Many of our winter bird visitors come from north-western lands like Eastern Europe and Siberia. To avoid flying over the skyscraper peaks of the Himalayas, they come in through the Indus valley and 'turn left' into the land blob of the Gujarat peninsula. So, in 1960, Sálim Bhai and his team from the BNHS were in the burning desert, setting up nets in preparation for the first wave of migrant birds.

The BNHS had, in the past, had a few very startling 'recoveries' of their rings, even from faraway Turkestan and Siberia. Ornithologists all over the world were becoming serious bird ringers, and the technology had advanced. The early nets to trap the birds had been heavy and difficult to manage. Since then, the Japanese had invented 'mist nets', which were light and springy, somewhat like giant spiderwebs.

Next question: where should these nets be put up? A place had to be found where the migrants would 'picnic' for a day or two – rest, eat, drink –

before their next long flight. Done. But as soon as the tents were pitched and the camp got going, there was a sudden, heavy, early monsoon, bringing flood and famine. It was difficult to work in that large swamp, or even to find food for the bird team.

Still, the success of this camp was that the ornithologists from the BNHS learnt to use the mist nets. An expert had especially come from Switzerland to show them how to put up the long, almost invisible nets on bamboo poles. Even the keen eyesight of birds missed its hair-thin strands of nylon. Imagining it is flying into a bush, or patch of grass, the bird finds itself bouncing about in a hammock. Being springy and elastic, the net doesn't hurt or damage the bird. But the bird must be quickly untangled, weighed, measured and ringed. Then it is free to fly away, wondering what on earth that noise and excitement had been about.

The camp was a real bird haven, but unfortunately, it was also a favourite spot for snakes. It was infested by saw-scaled vipers, deadly venomous snakes that move fast and are quick to strike. The snake's sandy colouring makes it blend in so well with the desert soil that it's easy to step on. Sálim Bhai had brought along an antivenom serum kit and on the first evening they tried to follow the instructions. But they were so complicated that it was decided that in case of a bite, they should be kind to the victim and allow him to die peacefully! Fortunately, no one was bitten in spite of some close shaves.

These bird-ringing camps became an important part of the work of Sálim Bhai and the BNHS. Millions of birds were ringed in many parts of the country, and the 'recoveries' (rings returned to the BNHS) began to tell, for the first time, the story of where and how migratory birds fly.

The chief and most important ringing centre was Bharatpur in Rajasthan, which is today a national park, thanks to Sálim Bhai. Bharatpur is a large wetland where millions of migrant waterfowl and other birds arrive every winter. One of these is the rare and beautiful Siberian crane. It is also home to many species of waterbirds, such as storks, herons, spoonbills and ibises, which breed here and then migrate locally, within India; they are 'domestic tourists'. Very little was known about their movements as well.

This bird paradise was the private hunting ground of the royal family of Bharatpur. Their VIP guests were 'entertained' by mass massacres of waterbirds, which were kept moving by beaters, making them easy targets. There are records of 3,000 and 4,000 birds shot in a single day! But the real danger to Bharatpur came after Independence when the local farmers and politicians tried, and almost succeeded, in getting this fantastic birdhouse drained and converted into agricultural land. This would have been the end of one of the most precious waterbird sanctuaries in the world. Fortunately, Sálim Bhai, who knew Prime Minister Nehru personally and also knew of his deep love for nature, asked him to stop this crazy plan. And Nehru did. Today, ornithologists and tourists come from all over the world to watch the teeming bird life of Bharatpur.

Sálim Ali (second from left) with botanist and entomologist Mary Livingstone Ripley and ornithologist Sidney Dillon Ripley (next to him, on right) on a bird collection trip

A RARE SPECIES OF UNCLE

SÁLIM BHAI WAS MY MAMOO, my grandmother Kamoo's brother. By the time I was born, he was living with Kamoo and her husband Hassan – our Nani and Nana – in Bandra, Bombay. My parents were both nature lovers, and my father Zafar Futehally became interested in birds through Sálim Mamoo. They worked closely together at the BNHS, and both my father and mother visited the famous bird camps. My mother Laeeq wrote a book with Sálim Mamoo, called *Common Indian Birds.* Quite often, when new birdwatchers are out in the field, one or two of them are anxiously looking into my mother's book, trying to identify a bird.

My brother, sister and I grew up in a very nature-friendly atmosphere. At dinner, we often heard words like habitat and ecosystem and erosion and bird ringing and black-winged kite. Many discussions about environmental issues took place around our beautiful old dining table in Juhu Lane, Andheri. It seated and fed famous naturalists including Sir Peter Scott and Dr George Schaller.

I greatly envied my school friends because they could sleep as late as they liked on weekends. We, on the other hand, were woken up at 5:30 a.m. on a Saturday or Sunday to go birdwatching at Borivali Park, which is now a national park. Sometimes Sálim Mamoo would come along, too. He'd drive his Willys Jeep – the present from Loke Wan Tho – like a battle tank, honking and shouting at every person and car on the road. His temper, never very sweet, was definitely at its worst on the road. As passengers, we learnt to shut our eyes and hope for the best. I was in one of his 'small' accidents once when he was driving me to school. He hit a bullock cart, luckily not causing any damage or injuries, and shouted at the poor victim so loudly that the bullock-cart driver began to apologize, forgetting that it was entirely Sálim Mamoo's fault.

At Borivali, we had favourite walking trails in the forest, following pretty, fern-fringed streams and waterfalls. During the monsoon, there was water everywhere, and plenty of harbours for our paper boats (many made from my undone homework sheets). I was not a great birdwatcher and still remain very ignorant. I keep buying bird books and binoculars, hoping that these will magically make me clever. But Sálim Mamoo definitely had some secret bird-finding machinery in his brain. He could see what no one else saw, hear what no one else heard, and walk more miles than could others much younger than he. Even when an old man, he'd ride a camel or pony, walk for hours in the hot sun, climb up a shaky ladder to peer into a bird's nest. He could go without water the whole day on a desert trek.

My sister and I often went to stay with our Nani and Nana at 46 Pali Hill and 'our' bedroom, the guest room, was directly above Sálim Mamoo's apartment. He had a large study and library, with a bathroom and a small bedroom behind it. In the summer, he often slept outside, with his trusty old .22 long rifle leaning against a tree trunk nearby, to discourage robbers from coming too close.

We always hoped madly that Sálim Mamoo would be away in some jungle or mountain or desert (and he often was). We loved to play hide-and-seek with our cousins, and Sálim Mamoo didn't like noise when he was working. What's the fun of hide-and-seek if you can't yell and shriek? When he came up the steps to tell us to be quiet, we'd all dive under the beds in fright. But our feet sticking out, and our nervous giggles, would give us away.

Of course, *we* had to put up with the noise of his typewriter at five in the morning. Clack, clack, clack. There were no silent computers then. He typed most of his books himself; it was only after he had started work on the 10-volume *Handbook of the Birds of India and Pakistan* that he had a typist to help him. When I see his *Book of Indian Birds*, I still grumble to myself: hey, you really robbed us of sleep, didn't you?

However busy the birds were keeping him, Sálim Mamoo tried to make it to Kihim every May. Kihim, a beach around 100 kilometres south of Bombay, is our family's summer haven. On a 4-kilometre stretch of beach are about 15 homes belonging to our aunts, uncles and cousins. Kihim is actually more than a summer haven. It's more like a sort of religion. To us, the word Kihim means peace and quiet, fun and friendship, and fantastic natural beauty. All these drew Sálim Mamoo to Kihim. But perhaps the most powerful magnet for him – and for all of us – were the basketfuls of *aphoos* or Alphonso, the king of mangoes. This king is sweeter, nobler and greater than any human king ever was or ever will be. We pretend that we go to Kihim to meet our extended family, but actually we're all there to meet (and eat) the king.

Sálim Mamoo loved to wander in the forest and paddy fields inland of the beach. This is where he'd done his famous weaver bird or baya study, and it remained his lifelong retreat. When Nani and Nana died, and the Pali Hill house was sold, Sálim Mamoo moved to Kihim, and spent his last days there.

Fortunately for us noisy children, Sálim Mamoo loved young people. He was certainly a scolder, like all grown-ups are, but the next minute he'd lasso our necks with his hooked walking stick and make a funny face. There was always laughter when he was around, and his was the loudest and most croaky. Once, my cousin and I decided to bake a cake for him on his birthday. It came out looking like a small, rocky hill. However, we carried it proudly to the table and the 62-year-old 'birthday boy' was told to cut it. After a short struggle, the cake fell on the floor – with a thud! Sálim Mamoo sprang back and peered at the cake. 'Strange,' he said, 'it didn't break! Lucky it didn't fall on my foot.'

Sálim Mamoo had a great passion for motorcycles, and his nieces and nephews were sometimes given rides in the sidecar of his 500 cc Sunbeam, on which he had travelled widely in Europe in 1950. That year there was an ornithological meeting in Sweden and Sálim Mamoo decided to arrive on his motorbike.

It went with him by ship to England, where Colonel Meinertzhagen was standing on a wooden crate so his short Indian friend would be able to see him in the crowd. Then it was off on motorbike to Sweden, Germany and France, meeting old birdwatcher friends. Both the Sunbeam and its master enjoyed the adventure immensely, in spite of a 'full toss' now and then.

The Sunbeam was famous in Pali Hill traffic until, at the age of 68, Sálim Mamoo sadly gave it up. By that time, none of us were too happy about accepting invitations to go for a ride, afraid that it would be our last one. But the Bird Man roared through the crazy Bombay roads, wriggling in and out through the traffic fearlessly. Fear and he were strangers. He was always ready to try his luck. Even, once, with a man-eating tiger.

It was during the Bastar survey. On a very bad road about 30 kilometres from the nearest town, the Jeep broke down. Other traffic, mostly bullock carts, had been stopped because there was a man-eating tiger in the area. Having waited all day for a lift, Sálim Bhai decided to take things into his own hands – or, rather, feet.

At midnight, he set off with an equally brave bird skinner, a loaded gun on his shoulder. The forest they walked through was exactly where the tiger had had his last human meal a few days before. In that thick jungle, in a sudden attack, they may well have ended up nourishing the tiger. No time to unshoulder the gun, aim and fire. After a six-hour march in darkness, they reached the town and were told their trek had been absolute madness. But the Jeep did get repaired, and the survey continued.

Both in Bombay and in Kihim, Sálim Mamoo had a small army of followers, many of them children interested in wildlife. Because of him, many people in our family became converts to the religion of natural history and conservation. I believe this kind of person is sometimes called a 'wildlifer'. Some study wildlife and the environment, others are serious birdwatchers, and yet others lead treks and hikes into forests. I have many memories of Sálim Mamoo, binoculars around his neck, surrounded by little birdwatchers, mouths open, staring into space.

But most of all I remember the joy on his face when he was looking at a bird. It didn't have to be a rare or colourful one. Even a bee-eater or drongo brought a special light into his wrinkled, sunburnt face. Birdwatching was his religion, his road to peace.

THE CALL OF THE BIRD MAN

SÁLIM ALI DIED IN 1987 at the age of 90, but he left such a strong legacy that it feels like he is still around. The work he started was so timely and important that it kept going, kept growing. Let's look at a few things he left behind, which continue to add value to our lives today.

Birdwatching, now a common 'timepass' activity or serious hobby or even career, was a barely known word when he was a young man. He gave us the gift of birdwatching, with its range of involvement from fun to research. In parks, forests, lakes and other wilderness areas, it is common to see people – children and adults – with binoculars around their necks, excitedly pointing at a bird on a tree or electric pole. Thanks to Sálim Ali, an exciting new option has been added to outdoor activities in India. For outdoorsy people, birdwatching is hard to beat and needs minimal equipment; and often, a keen eyesight can replace binoculars.

There are now birdwatching clubs and informal bird groups all over the country. Group birding has caught on and many birders, both amateurs and experts, look for these when they move to another town or city. Our big cities such as Bengaluru, Chennai and Mumbai each have many such clubs, with the more knowledgeable birders guiding and encouraging the others, taking them under their wing, so to speak. There is, therefore, great camaraderie and fellow feeling among birders, and many strong and lasting friendships have developed while following and watching our feathered friends.

And then there's *The Book of Indian Birds*, in such common use by the 'birderatti' that it's referred to as 'the bird book', or simply by his name: 'I'll bring my Sálim Ali along,' one says. It was our first field guide to Indian birds and, dare I say this, remains the best, an opinion shared by many serious ornithologists. This is a valuable legacy indeed, and the one that required the most work because it was our first field guide for birds, requiring extensive research and discovery. It meant walking miles and miles every day, observing birds for hours and hours, and conducting meticulous research for years and years.

Apart from the information on our birds and their habitat, *The Book of Indian Birds* gives us another great gift: Sálim Ali's elegant and precise writing, which many have tried to emulate. His choice of word and phrase is so exact that a mental image is

The north-eastern Himalayan forest thrush (*Zoothera salimalii*) named after Sálim Ali

created of the colours, shape and movements of the bird, and often the call as well. He was, in a way, the creator of popular science writing in India. Journalists who specialize in this field of writing and reporting talk about how helpful it is to read the book for its language.

We have many Protected Areas (PAs) that resulted from Sálim Ali's relentless campaigns among politicians and officials. These include the Silent Valley National Park in Kerala and the Bharatpur Bird Sanctuary in Rajasthan. Other such PAs are named after him, such as the estuarine Dr Sálim Ali Bird Sanctuary on the western tip of the island of Chorao along the River Mandovi in Goa; another Sálim Ali Bird Sanctuary spread over 25 kilometres of the Western Ghats in Munnar, Kerala; the third Sálim Ali Bird Sanctuary, around 13 kilometres from Kothamangalam, also in Kerala; the Sálim Ali National Park in Srinagar, Jammu and Kashmir; and more.

Fauna and flora named after him includes the north-eastern Himalayan forest thrush (*Zoothera*

The entrance to the bird sanctuary named after Sálim Ali in Goa

salimalii), discovered almost three decades after his death by a group of international ornithologists led by Upsala University, Sweden, and Sálim Ali's fruit bat (*Latidens salimalii*), first described in 1948 but later correctly identified and named by Thai ornithologist and mammologist Kitti Thonglongya.

Institutions connected to ornithology and conservation have also taken on the Sálim Ali brand name, such as the Sálim Ali Centre for Ornithology and Natural History (SACON), a national centre for information, education and research in ornithology and natural history in India and hailed as a 'centre of excellence' of the Government of India's Ministry of Environment and Forests, and the Sálim Ali School of Ecology and Environmental Sciences at the Pondicherry University. Mumbai now has a Sálim Ali Chowk, and the Indian Postal Department has released two stamps to honour him.

Stamps honouring Sálim Ali

Birding activities and competitions have become regular features, like the annual Sálim Ali Bird Count, a citizen science pan-country census, which starts around 12 November, his birthday.

However, in my opinion the most powerful part of Sálim Bhai's legacy is the true meaning of conservation in the Indian, or indeed any context. He was against the 'sentimental brigade', who equate conservation with animal welfare and protection rather than a rational and empirical science. Such people block effective conservation practices such as removal of harmful, invasive species of plants and animals. Sálim Bhai believed that there was a population explosion in some species, which was causing severe damage, such as crows (to other birds and their eggs and fledglings) and parakeets (to agriculture).

It's time to hear Sálim Bhai's voice and words at a deeper level, before it's too late, about this and other messages: preserving rather than trashing what's left of our wilderness areas; batting for science over sentiment in conservation; and eschewing overt materialism and consumerism. As a role model for past and current generations of Indians, the Bird Man of India is beyond par. So, let's pick up our binocs and give a loud shout-out for the birds and their conservation...which includes their habitat – which, incidentally, is ours as well.

BIRDS AND US

MANY YEARS AGO in China, during the Cultural Revolution (around 1966 to June 1976), the government decided to kill off sparrows, because they destroy crops. But when all the sparrows were killed, there was a huge explosion in the population of insect pests. The Chinese had forgotten that though sparrows eat grain, they also eat insects – many of which are pests that are the main enemy of the farmer. In the same way, fishermen gnash their teeth at crocodiles because these poor reptiles eat fish. But this is just half the story. Crocodiles also chomp up the big predator fish that feed on the smaller species, or the type of fish we make curries out of. So, like birds, they do a bit of harm to humans, but a whole lot of good.

Birds have lovely calls and songs, they don't bite, and they are beautiful. (Except the poor crow, which is neither colourful nor tuneful.) The songs and colours of birds have inspired great poetry, music and art. Even common birds like the kingfisher and woodpecker look as though they were especially made for an exhibition.

However, birds, as we saw with the story of the sparrows, were not put on Earth just for our enjoyment. They are one of the most critical, or important, links in the complex web of life that we call the environment. They are master pollinators who transfer pollen from place to place. Many seeds do not germinate unless they are first eaten and digested by birds, so they are wonderful seed carriers, too. In this way, birds make forests.

Certain species of birds pollinate certain species of plants. Similarly, one kind of bird may have a particular liking for one type of insect, perhaps an insect harmful to humans or crops. Every bird plays a crucial, unique part in its habitat, which is the area it lives in. Some birds like living near streams, some in the mountains, some in trees in cities. But many species of birds are discovering, with surprise, that human beings want to take over their habitat.

These 'Terminator' creatures cut down forests, pollute rivers and streams, build dams that change rivers, and use powerful pesticides that kill everything for miles around. The smallest Terminator action causes big environmental distress. When we greedily chop down old forest trees, for example, bole-nesting birds become homeless. A bole is a hole in a tree trunk; owls live in them, and many other species as well. The Malabar hornbill, one of our most spectacular and interesting birds, nests in the boles of old, tall trees in evergreen forests. The male hornbill 'locks' his wife and babies in the nest by covering the opening with mud. He leaves a small kitchen-doorway through which he feeds his family insects, lizards, snakes and other delicious treats. This way, the chicks are safe from predators but get their daily meals and snacks on time.

Now such old forest trees are becoming rare. Wood poachers are cutting them down for their valuable wood; others are clearing forests for the kind of 'development' we like: crowded cities, dangerous highways, bigger and faster cars, and more pollution. Thus, we destroy not just birds and other wildlife, but ourselves as well. It's kind of silly to be chopping down your own home, isn't it? Ornithologists are worried about the future of many birds, including the hornbill; it is certainly not going to change its nesting habits to suit human needs. Hornbills are one of the many species of birds that may not be able to survive human beings.

We know so much more today about our birds, largely because of Sálim Ali and his associates. We know something about their nesting, eating and roosting or sleeping habits, and about their travel

plans for the Christmas holidays. We know about the behaviour of different species: we know their special calls or the song each of them sings. We also know the places they are likely to be found, or their distribution. For example, the tern, which looks like an origami project, is a beach and ocean enthusiast, and wouldn't be found in a forest. The star singer, the shama, however, sticks to its thick forest home.

So much is still to be discovered: both for the sake of increasing our knowledge as well as to help conserve certain rare species. Because of the criminal overuse of pesticides, some birds are becoming rare. Can you guess why? The chemicals in pesticides 'thin' the birds' eggshell, which breaks before the baby is ready to hatch. Many countries have banned the use of certain pesticides that are dangerous to birds. In India, many birds that were once common in certain areas, are disappearing. We need to find out why, and do something about it – urgently.

Fortunately, thousands of bird fans are working hard to try and conserve the birds of our country. They include amateur birdwatchers as well as serious, elderly, experienced ornithologists, many of whom were encouraged and helped by Sálim Bhai in the past, or are inspired by him. Thanks to his studies and work, these new ornithologists have many more resources to help them than he did.

If you are interested in birds, you too can help in the very important effort to study and conserve birds. You can do this even if you're a young student: in fact, all the better, as you can be more active, and cover more miles than the older birdwatchers. You can climb trees to spy on nests (but don't let the crows see you!) and scramble up thorny slopes after an interesting-looking bird. Unlike many hobbies, this is not an expensive one, and can be done anywhere. You may live near the sea or in the mountains or near a forest, or even in the middle of the city. The good news about birds is that they are always around.

If you can get a pair of binoculars, great. But don't pester your parents for this unless you are absolutely sure that you are seriously interested. A pair of young eyes is capable of many useful discoveries! Keep a small notebook and pencil or pen handy whenever you go 'birding', and write down every observation meticulously, starting with the date, time and location. And of course, you need a reference book, and the best one is *The Book of Indian Birds.* Or, perhaps you have a friend or neighbour who knows the common birds of your area, and you could use them as your first resource.

Pester them! Ask questions! Start by learning the names of 10 common birds, and try and add a new one every day, or every week, depending on how much time you can spare. Make a bird list every time you go on a bird walk. And don't be discouraged if you find yourself writing down 'crow' and 'sparrow' a lot. These are birds, too! Soon, your list may include slightly less common ones, like the golden oriole, tree pie and kingfisher.

As you become more and more interested (and, hopefully, knowledgeable), try and find other birders you can go out with, and learn from. Most Indian cities, and even small towns, now have birdwatching clubs, and you should find one you like, and join up. It's amazing how much knowledge is locked away in the heads of a group of 'amateur' birders. You will find yourself learning a lot. Birdwatchers are also nice people to know, and you will make some good friends through the good offices of birds.

One day, you will find you have become a birdwatcher. You will recognize all the common, and some uncommon, birds of your area, know something about their personal and public lives, and have heated arguments with other birders about whether 'it' is a wren or lark...or leaf. At this point, you can start writing little articles about your observations, and sending these to ornithological

magazines or websites, or posting them on a blog of your own. However, make sure that your observation is of interest, and well written. It is no fun to get a rejection letter from an editor.

More than anything else, keep your eyes and ears peeled. As Whistler told Sálim Bhai, question everything. Why is this bird in the hot sun at midday; what's it trying to do? Why have these two been fluttering around that bush for hours; could they be nesting? What's that funny squawk; is a bird being attacked by that large rat snake…? And so on.

Don't forget that an important discovery about sparrows was made by a young boy. If you are curious enough, you could well be another Sálim Ali.